Weekly Reader Children's Book Club presents

Twenty-Five Dragons

WEEKLY READER
CHILDREN'S BOOK CLUB

This is a registered trademark

Twenty-Five

Illustrated by Joann Daley

Dragons

Eleanor Coerr

FOLLETT PUBLISHING COMPANY
CHICAGO

Dedicated to Wym, Robert and Bill.

ISBN 0 695-40179-3 Titan binding
ISBN 0 695-80179-1 Trade binding

Library of Congress Catalog Card Number: 75-121412

Weekly Reader Children's Book Club Edition
Intermediate Division

Chapter One
Chi Fu's First Mistake

It was the first time in all of his ten years that Chi Fu had been chased by a policeman. He ran as fast as he could down the streets of Taipei toward the marketplace where he could hide easily. The market, with its hundreds of stalls selling everything from rice to furniture, was the best place for a Chinese boy in trouble.

The policeman waved his stick and yelled, "Stop, thief! Stop, thief!" as he pounded after Chi Fu. People turned to stare at the frightened boy as he fairly flew down the busy street, darting in and out of traffic.

Chi Fu looked back and put on an extra spurt of speed. The policeman was so close he could almost reach out and grab the collar of

Chi Fu's dark blue school uniform. He streaked across the street and pushed into the middle of a crowd of buyers in the marketplace. Where should he hide? He frantically dodged behind a stall loaded with lettuce; then, with one eye

on the policeman, scurried toward a pile of large straw baskets—just the place!

The policeman was slowly walking around each stall, looking into every nook and corner. Since it was midafternoon by now, there were many mothers with their children buying food for supper, and every boy in a school uniform looked very much like Chi Fu. Chi Fu cautiously peeped around a basket and saw the puzzled policeman scratching his head as he tried to decide which boy to chase.

Chi Fu quietly crept inside a large basket and turned it over on top of himself. For the first time since the chase began he was able to catch his breath, but danger was not over yet. For a long time Chi Fu listened tensely to the footsteps and voices outside the basket. Finally, when nobody paused to ask about a runaway boy, his heart gradually stopped beating so hard and he settled down for a long wait.

Since Chi Fu had nothing to do in his basket but think, he went over the events that had brought him there. He had started off on the wrong foot when he listened to his friend in school during the lunch hour.

"It's the most beautiful bicycle I've ever seen," his friend Chen Wu had said, "and it is sitting right out on the sidewalk in front of Mr. Wang's store."

Every boy in school knew about Mr. Wang's store, because he sold the best bicycles in Taipei.

The more Chen Wu talked about the bicycle, the more Chi Fu wanted it; this was the one he had dreamed about all his life. In a flash he made up his mind to go into Taipei and see it that very afternoon—in fact, that very moment. When he had finished eating the lunch of rice and fish his mother had prepared for him, Chi Fu started off toward Taipei.

"Hey!" yelled his friend. "Where are you going? Come back!"

But Chi Fu only waved and grinned, his black eyes twinkling with mischief as he hurried to get away from the school grounds before the bell rang. His teacher, Miss Wu, would indeed be angry, but Chi Fu did not want to think about that; he just wanted to think about red bicycles.

Now that he looked back on it, he was as surprised as Chen Wu had been at his own disobedience. Usually Chi Fu was a very good student and never caused his teacher any trouble. Besides that, he was never allowed to go into the city without permission from his family.

Chi Fu's thoughts were broken when he heard a snuffling sound outside the basket. Through a crack in the weave he could see a dog trying to make friends with him and whining softly.

"Go away!" he whispered. "Shoo!"

If the dog started to bark, Chi Fu knew he would be caught. For an agonizing few minutes the dog tried to push his nose under the basket, but Chi Fu held it down tightly with both hands.

When the dog finally gave up, Chi Fu sagged with relief and wiped the perspiration from his forehead. Phew! That had been a close call.

Then he remembered how beautiful the bicycle looked. There it had been, right in front of Mr. Wang's store like an important statue, its shiny red body gleaming in the sunshine. Chi Fu had put his school books in the wire basket and quickly climbed into the seat. He just had to see what it felt like to sit on such a beauty —if only for a moment.

As he sat there under the basket, a shiver of pleasure tingled up and down Chi Fu's spine when he thought of the cold feel of it, the perfect way the pedals fit his feet, and the fine rubber handlebars.

The terrible thing had happened while Chi Fu had been sitting on that bicycle.

Chapter Two
A Wild Ride

In his excitement, Chi Fu had accidentally pushed the support away, and the bicycle rolled down the steep street—with him in the saddle.

Mr. Wang had run out of his shop yelling, "Stop! Help! Police! Stop that boy!"

Chi Fu went faster and faster. The wind whistled around his ears and his feet waved in the air as he tried to find the whirling pedals. Drivers of cars and pedicabs honked their horns and angrily shouted, "Get off the street! Get

out of the way!" Chi Fu hung on for dear life as he sped on toward a street crossing. Chi Fu closed his eyes tight and waited for the crash; he would surely hit one of the cars that streamed along the road at the bottom of the hill.

But no, luck was with him. An oxcart filled with straw was parked by the sidewalk with its back door down. Chi Fu was heading straight for it, but he couldn't stop and didn't have time to swerve. The bicycle raced on and sailed into the open back end of the cart. The next thing Chi Fu knew he was sitting in the middle of the straw brushing wisps of it out of his eyes.

During the moments of confusion that followed, while the oxcart held up traffic and drivers shouted and waved their arms, Chi Fu grabbed his books, jumped out of the wagon, and ran as fast as he could go. That is how he ended up in a basket in the marketplace.

He sighed deeply in the darkness of the basket. Now he was in for real trouble. It would be late before he dared to show his face and go home, and when he got there he would be punished for missing school and going into Taipei without permission.

Chi Fu had fallen fast asleep when someone lifted the basket. He instantly awoke and anxiously looked around for the policeman, but the marketplace was almost empty, and all the merchants were packing up for the night.

The basket seller—a kindly old fellow with a white beard—looked searchingly into Chi Fu's face. "Why are you hiding, boy?" he asked. "I'm sure you haven't done anything wrong. Come now, run on home before it gets too late."

He slipped an orange into Chi Fu's hand and gave him a little push toward the street. Chi Fu was so surprised by the sudden kindness of the old man that tears stung his eyes. He politely murmured, "Thank you," and started off toward home.

It had certainly not been an ordinary day, but then Chi Fu was not an ordinary boy. He was called a clay-boy. All the men in the Li family had been clay-men for hundreds of years.

Since his father had died a few years before, Chi Fu's grandfather was teaching him the ancient art of making birds and flowers out of clay.

Chi Fu lived with Grandfather Li, his mother, and his sister, Little Yu Mei, on the green island of Taiwan. Their house sat at the very foot of Grass Mountain, just outside the bustling city of Taipei.

Every morning Chi Fu watched Grandfather Li prepare to go into Taipei by tying a folding table and stool onto his bicycle. He worked all day making and selling his clay objects, moving from street to street with his equipment. People liked to watch his clever fingers transform the clay into realistic flowers and birds that almost sang.

More than anything else in the world Chi Fu wanted his own bicycle so that he could ride into Taipei and work beside Grandfather Li. Whenever Chi Fu talked about this, Grandfather Li always said, "When you are old enough to earn money for a bicycle, you will be old enough to go into Taipei and work with me."

It was a long walk home and the street lights were twinkling in the dusk when Chi Fu turned into the yard. The house, with its adobe walls and red-tiled roof, had never looked better to him. When he passed between the clumps of bamboo that made a fence for the yard, Chi Fu saw that his whole family was waiting for him. They were sitting together on a long bench facing the road watching a duck and three chickens scratch around in the dirt at their feet.

His mother put her arms around him and squeezed him tightly, and Little Yu Mei grabbed his hand. But Grandfather Li sternly led Chi Fu through the central living room, which was also the kitchen, and into Chi Fu's bedroom. He scolded in a quiet voice: he told Chi Fu that all good Chinese children tried to please their parents and grandparents, that he had let them down. The quieter Grandfather Li's voice became, the worse Chi Fu felt. He tried to explain what had happened, how he hadn't meant to do any harm; but he knew all the time he had been unkind, especially to his mother.

Every summer evening Chi Fu and his family would sit in the yard, enjoying the cool breeze after the heat of the day until it was time for bed. Sometimes Grandfather Li told exciting

stories about the old life in China, and other times they just sat together feeling happy and content. This evening Chi Fu had to stay in his bedroom alone for punishment. As the soft voices of his family wafted in through the open window, he made up his mind not to do anything to worry his mother again.

But that was before the twenty-five dragons came into his life.

Chapter Three
Twenty-five Dragons

The next day Chen Wu met Chi Fu at the school door and whispered, "I think Miss Wu noticed that you skipped classes yesterday."

Chi Fu kept his head down in the classroom, too ashamed to look into Miss Wu's face. He slouched down in his seat, hoping she wouldn't notice him, but the first thing she did was call on Chi Fu to give a short talk about his trip to Taipei the day before.

Everyone giggled as Chi Fu slowly got to

his feet, his face burning, and stared miserably straight ahead. The class bully, Tao Chi, kept grinning and making faces as Chi Fu tried to think of something to say.

Finally, Miss Wu said, "You may sit down, Chi Fu, and stay in after school to write a composition about your afternoon in Taipei."

After writing several pages, Chi Fu got permission to go home. Outside in the yard Chen Wu was patiently waiting to walk home with him.

"Tell me about the bicycle," Chen Wu asked eagerly, "and all the things that happened to you in Taipei."

Chi Fu started to describe the red bicycle, but he didn't say more than a few words before Tao Chi swaggered up and yelled, "Hey, Chi Fu! What are you looking at bicycles for? You'll never have enough money to buy one."

He grabbed a button on Chi Fu's jacket and yanked it off. "Here—use this for money," he sneered, and threw the button in Chi Fu's face. This attack made Chi Fu so angry that he swung blindly at Tao Chi, who was about twice his size. Tao Chi gave him a hefty shove that knocked him down and walked off.

"I'll really hit you hard next time," the bully yelled in parting.

Chi Fu got up and Chen Wu brushed the dust off his uniform. "Don't pay any attention to him," he said, "Tao Chi is the meanest boy in the whole world."

Chi Fu agreed with him as he looked at the big tear in his jacket, but he soon forgot about it when he started telling his friend all the strange things that had happened to him in the city. Chen Wu's eyes grew rounder and rounder as Chi Fu talked. It sounded like an adventure out of a book.

After swearing he would never tell anyone about the runaway bicycle, Chen Wu went on home while Chi Fu settled down to practice his clay art the way other boys practice the piano or play baseball. He took a box of clay out into the sunny yard and sat down in the cool shade where his table always sat. Chi Fu tried to remember how many years he had been learning to make flowers and birds out of clay, but his memory didn't go back that far. Probably ever since he could hold anything in his hands. Little Yu Mei, the three brown chickens, and the duck watched him, as they always did.

First, Chi Fu put lumps of different colored clay in a neat row on his table. There were balls of all his favorite colors: the red of his sister's hair ribbon, the finest jade green, the blue of a morning sky, and the warm yellow of sunshine. He also used black as black as his own hair and white as pure as gardenia petals. The clay was a secret mixture that Grandfather Li said was made of rice flour, clay from the earth, salt, water, and a pinch of dried dragon's blood. The trick was in knowing how much of each to use and, after the clay objects dried in the sun, they would be hard enough for children to play with.

Next, Chi Fu pressed a small ball of red clay onto the end of a bamboo stick like a chopstick. He carefully flattened some red and white clay into a strip. Chi Fu cut it with scissors in exactly the right places and wound the strip around the small ball of clay. A push here, a pull there and—presto!—a peony bloomed on the stick.

Little Yu Mei said, "Ah-h-h!" and the

chickens cackled with admiration.

Chi Fu could make hundreds of peonies, and they would be exactly alike, right down to the last petal and leaf. He could also make chrysanthemums, lotus blossoms, and all kinds of birds.

Usually he felt proud of his work, but today he did not. Chi Fu was so tired of making the same things the same way, day after day, month after month, that he decided to do something he had never done before.

As soon as he saw his mother go down the street to the grocery store to buy vegetables for dinner, he winked at Little Yu Mei and said, "How would you like to watch me make something different?"

His sister's dark eyes opened wide with surprise. She had never heard Chi Fu talk like this before.

"Can you make anything—anything at all?"

"You name it," Chi Fu boasted, "and I'll make it with my magic clay."

He picked up the lump of red clay and gaily tossed it into the air. "What would you like to see? A grand temple with a red roof? Devils with funny faces?"

Little Yu Mei was quiet for a moment; then she laughed. "I'll bet you can't make a dragon."

"Ho!" Chi Fu said. "Just watch me."

His hands flew as he pulled and cut and rolled the clay into shape. Before long he held up a bright red dragon with a yellow tail and snappy black eyes, perched on top of a bamboo stick.

"That one looks important," Little Yu Mei said happily. "He must be the Dragon King himself. Now make his helpers."

Every Chinese boy and girl knows many stories about the Dragon King and his twenty-four helpers. High in the clouds they live in a glittering palace. When the dragons are in good humor, they bring sunny weather to Taiwan; but when they are grumpy, they knock the clouds about, breathe fire onto them until they are burnt gray, scatter lightning across the sky, and make rain pour down in buckets.

Chi Fu quickly made another dragon, and it was even wilder than the first: this one was blue with green dots. He kept on building clay dragons, and each one was different.

Little Yu Mei pushed the bamboo sticks into the soft earth until she had a garden of dragons growing there. It was the first time Chi Fu had ever made dragons, and it was also the first time he had ever disobeyed Grandfather Li. Chi Fu knew he was supposed to make flowers and birds every day and not waste precious time. He had completely forgotten his promise the night before to be good.

The two children were having so much fun they did not hear Grandfather Li wheel his bicycle into the yard. He spoke in a voice as cold as ice. "How dare you sit and waste your practice time on dragons. You'll never become a true clay artist that way."

Little Yu Mei ran into the kitchen, the ribbons on her pigtails bobbing up and down. The three chickens and the duck waddled after her and hid underneath the table.

"I'm sorry, sir." Chi Fu's voice was low. "I just got tired of making flowers."

There was a long silence.

Chi Fu finally went on, "You did tell us that it is hard to sell flowers and birds these days."

"It is better to sell for small profits than fail in business," Grandfather Li said sternly, "and that is exactly what you would do. Who in the world would buy clay dragons?"

Chi Fu timidly looked up into Grandfather Li's angry face. "If Little Yu Mei liked them, perhaps mothers would buy some to make their children laugh."

"Aiyee!" Grandfather Li sighed and shook his head. "It is easier to rule a country than to raise a good boy. Now take those dragons apart before they dry so that you can use the clay again tomorrow," he ordered. Then he put his bicycle away, talking all the time about foolish young people who want to change the good old ways of doing things.

Chi Fu sadly took his dragons apart and put the pieces of clay back where they belonged in colored lumps and wrapped them in a wet cloth to keep them moist.

That night he stayed awake for a long time listening to the wind brush across the roof of the dark house. "If I had my own bicycle," Chi Fu thought, "maybe I could sell clay dragons and buy more food and clothes for all of us." He looked out the window at the black trees waving against the dark sky. They might even be able to go to the beach in the summer.

Chi Fu fell asleep with wonderful ideas like bright-colored balloons floating through his mind.

Chapter Four
Broom Trouble

The next day, while Miss Wu talked about division, multiplication, geography, and history, Chi Fu was thinking only about clay dragons and a red bicycle. They whirled around in his head. Chen Wu, who sat next to him, had to poke Chi Fu in the ribs three times to wake him up when it was his turn to answer Miss Wu's questions.

At last, school was over, and Chi Fu was first out the door and down the narrow path between green rice fields toward home. This time he did not practice in the sunny yard; he did something different. These days Chi Fu seemed to be doing something different all the time.

Chi Fu stopped at Mae's tiny store on the corner near his house. Mae sold toys, pencils, paper, comic books, and candy, and she always had time to talk to Chi Fu. He took a deep breath and said all at once, "I would like to earn enough money to buy a red bicycle. Do you need a boy like me to help you in the store?"

"Well, now," Mae said smiling, "I think I might have a job for such a boy."

Chi Fu's heart was pounding so hard he was sure she could hear it.

"Yes," she continued, "I could use a boy every afternoon for an hour or so." Mae handed him a broom. "You can start right now by sweeping the floor."

Chi Fu was so excited he forgot to thank her. He took the broom in both hands and began to sweep. He was going to show Mae that he could sweep harder and faster and better than anyone else.

Mae had gone into the back room when Chi Fu saw Tao Chi walk through the front door. His heart sank. He knew very well that

Tao Chi could not stand anyone being successful at anything.

"Hey, stupid," the bully jeered, "who ever taught you how to sweep a floor? I'll show you how to do it." He grabbed the broom and while the two boys were struggling, the broom handle crashed through a glass showcase. Pieces of glass showered over the floor.

"Try to explain that to Mae," Tao Chi yelled as he turned and ran.

Chi Fu looked hopelessly at the glass and couldn't manage to say a word when Mae rushed in. She looked glumly at the showcase and firmly took the broom away from Chi Fu. "You are a good boy, Chi Fu," she said gravely, "but I'm afraid you sweep too hard for a small shop like mine. Perhaps you could work better in Mr. Ching's garage across the street."

Chi Fu's well-worn sneakers scuffed up small clouds of dust as he gloomily walked down the path toward home.

"Are you feeling all right?" his mother asked with a worried frown. "You took a long

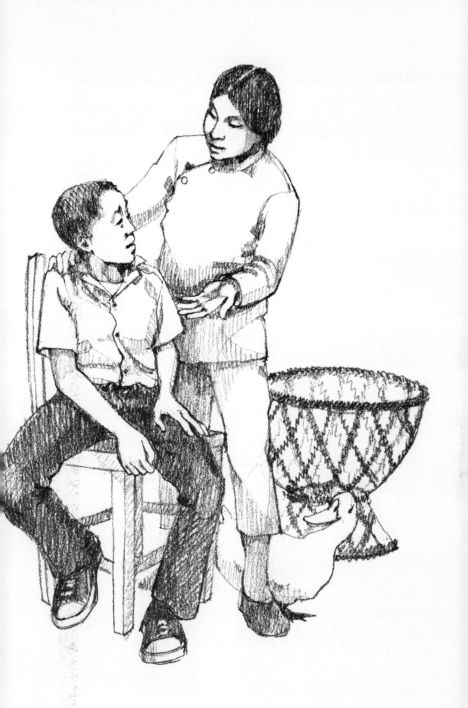

time coming home today, and you don't look well."

Chi Fu was silent for a moment; then he poured out his troubles, and told her everything.

"He is a real bully," she said, laying a hand lightly on Chi Fu's shoulder. "Don't mind him too much; you know why he does these things, don't you?"

Chi Fu looked up at his mother in surprise.

"Tao Chi is a lonely boy with no brothers and sisters and no friends," she explained. "Fighting is his only way of getting attention."

Knowing this did not make Chi Fu like him any better. He couldn't see why Tao Chi's loneliness gave him the right to make someone else unhappy, but he knew that his mother was trying to make him understand.

"I'm sorry about Tao Chi being lonely," Chi Fu said, "but he is still a bully, and I hate him."

In the evening, while the family sat outside listening to night sounds—the frogs croaking in the fields and the soft rustling of the leaves in the bamboo fence—Grandfather Li turned to Chi Fu and said, "If you want that bicycle so badly, I'll give you permission to stop practicing your clay art until you have earned enough money to buy it."

Chi Fu felt a warm glow of happiness. He was more determined than ever to get a job and as he drifted off to sleep he whispered to himself, "I will do it. I will get a job."

Chapter Five
Chi Fu's Job

The happy feeling was still with him in school all the next day. Even Tao Chi let him alone.

After classes Chi Fu ran as fast as he could to the garage across the street from Mae's shop. He stood in front of the garage for a while, trying to get up enough nerve to go in. Mr. Ching, a heavy, hard-muscled man, was fixing a motorcycle near the open door. He suddenly looked up and turned sharp black eyes on Chi Fu.

"Well, boy, what are you standing there for? Do you want something?"

Chi Fu cleared his throat to speak, but no sound came out.

"Do you want something or not? Speak up!"

"I—I need a job," Chi Fu said shyly. "I thought you might want someone to help you keep your garage clean."

Mr. Ching bent over the motorcycle again and continued tinkering with the engine. "As a matter of fact, I do need a boy; my helper quit yesterday. You can start in right now if you like."

"I'll take the job," Chi Fu said eagerly.

Mr. Ching pointed to a broom in the corner, and Chi Fu began to sweep the garage. He worked steadily until closing time.

"Good work," Mr. Ching said. "You keep it up, and we'll get along fine, just fine."

Chi Fu was so filled with joy he almost danced on the way home to supper. Grandfather Li gave him an approving pat on the back, and his mother smiled happily.

"You were fine," Little Yu Mei said. "I came and watched you for a while, but you didn't even see me."

"He was working too hard to see anyone," Grandfather Li chuckled.

Every afternoon Chi Fu hurried home from school to work in the garage. It was fun to clean the cars until they shone and fetch things for Mr. Ching. If he learned enough, Chi Fu was sure he could fix his new bicycle all by himself.

When news got around the class that Chi Fu had a job, Tao Chi lost no time coming to the garage. He lived nearby and liked to hang around the street, watching the cars and buses.

"Hey, you with the dirty face," he shouted. "How did a skinny kid like you get a man's job?"

Chi Fu angrily put up his fists, ready to fight, when Mr. Ching strode up to Tao Chi, grabbed him by the collar, and pushed him out into the street. "I'm warning you," he said icily, "keep out of my garage, or I'll give you more trouble than you bargained for."

For a couple of weeks life went along smoothly for Chi Fu, in spite of Tao Chi's constant teasing at school. He was doing the job well. It was hard, heavy work that made his arms and back ache every night, but when Chi Fu thought of the red bicycle, the pain melted away. He knew it might take almost a year to get that much money, and he was willing to wait.

Then, one day Mr. Ching stopped working, wiped his greasy hands on a cloth, and handed Chi Fu some money. "I want you to take the bus to Lu's machine shop in Taipei and bring back a parcel of tools for me. If you do it quickly, you can keep the change."

Chi Fu was so happy he ran out to the bus stop to get started as soon as possible. He would have gone home to ask permission to go into Taipei, but there wasn't time. Grandfather Li would surely understand and be pleased with the money Chi Fu hoped to bring home.

"Hey, just a minute!" yelled Mr. Ching. "You didn't wait to hear the address of the shop. How do you know where you are going?"

Chi Fu bit his lip. He carefully wrote down the name and address of the shop. When the big blue bus came roaring down Grass Mountain, he was the first to get on. He sat next to the window so he could watch for the right street. When the lady conductor called out the name of the street, he hopped off. So far, things were going well, and Chi Fu whistled a gay tune as he entered Lu's machine shop. He got the parcel and started back toward the bus stop.

Then he saw it. Mr. Wang's bicycle store was across the street. And there—right in front —was the same shiny red bicycle. He was glad it had not been scratched during the wild ride the other day. Chi Fu just had to go over and touch it—what harm could it do?

Chi Fu ran across the street and put his parcel down on the sidewalk so he could feel the bicycle with both hands. The metal was cold and smooth and new, just as he remembered it. He sat on the bicycle. This time he kept his

feet still so that he wouldn't go flying away again. How proud he would be to ride this bicycle to school! Wouldn't Tao Chi's eyes pop when he saw it! Nobody in his class had a bicycle as shiny and new as this one. And he could ride into Taipei with Grandfather Li and perhaps even sell some clay dragons.

With a sigh, Chi Fu got down and walked over to the bus stop, looking back at the bicycle with every step. It was not until he was on the bus that Chi Fu remembered the parcel. He pulled the cord and jumped down as soon as the bus stopped at the next corner. He ran all the way back to the bicycle shop.

The parcel was gone.

He did not dare ask Mr. Wang about the parcel, and certainly not the policeman who eyed him from the corner. They might recognize him as the boy who rode away with the bicycle.

All the way home Chi Fu was angry with himself and worried about what Mr. Ching would say. Grandfather Li was right. If he was not yet old enough to do a simple job, how could he be old enough to have a bicycle of his very own?

At the garage Mr. Ching frowned and said just what Chi Fu had expected. "Young man, I need someone I can depend upon. Perhaps you should stay home until you grow a little wiser." He did not pay Chi Fu, because the tools were worth much more than his salary.

There was a dull hotness in Chi Fu's stomach, and he wanted to hide inside Grass Mountain and let the tears come. He sadly walked home and prepared to practice his clay art again; there was nothing else to do now.

When his mother saw the look on Chi Fu's face, she seemed to know how he felt. She went on with her housework, waiting until he was ready to talk about it.

Chi Fu brought out the clay and slowly began to roll and snip and twirl it into birds and flowers. "Is it dragon time?" whispered Little Yu Mei. Chi Fu did not answer, but kept on making a red peony. This time his fingers did not move like lightning, and the flowers somehow did not look bright and cheery. Little Yu Mei, the three chickens, and duck felt sad, too, and soon stopped watching the clay-boy.

At suppertime Chi Fu couldn't eat a bite of the delicious fried fish and vegetables his mother had prepared. While Little Yu Mei chattered on as she always did, Chi Fu slipped away from the table and went to his room.

Later that evening his mother brought a bowl of steaming hot rice with milk and sat down beside him. She put her hands on his shoulders and looked deeply into his eyes.

"My son," she said softly, "you are trying to grow up too fast. Everyone makes mistakes, and you've made your first one out in the business world. It is painful, but it is how we learn."

Chi Fu blinked back the tears that pressed against his eyes and said, "I don't think I'll ever get that bicycle. Everything I do is wrong."

His mother pushed Chi Fu's straight hair back from his forehead and said, "Something you must learn now is that the bitter always comes first, then the sweet."

Chi Fu did not know when or how the sweet would come, but he hoped it would come soon.

There was still one place to go for a job and Chi Fu hurried there the first thing Saturday morning. When he left the house, the early mists had not yet risen, and Grass Mountain looked like a lumpy gray ghost in the distance.

The coal man was tall and strong and black with coal dust. When Chi Fu asked for a job, he put both hands on his hips and laughed, showing sparkling white teeth.

"Ho! Only strong men like me can lift coal every day."

Chi Fu stretched as tall as he could and held up his arm to show a bump of muscle. "I am strong, sir. Just give me a chance to show you."

"All right," the coal man said, still laughing. He pointed to two baskets bulging with coal. "Those go to a house down the road. Do you think you can carry them?"

Chi Fu had seen the coal man carrying coal

many times. He knew that a basket of coal was tied to each end of a bamboo pole that hung across his shoulders. It looked easy.

Chi Fu bent down and put the pole across his thin shoulders. Then he lifted and grunted and pulled until his muscles ached. Nothing happened. It was as if the baskets were nailed to the ground.

The coal man was right. Chi Fu was not yet old enough or strong enough to be a coal man's helper. At that moment the world looked as black as the coal in the basket to Chi Fu. He had tried to get another job and failed. Perhaps he wasn't good enough to do anything.

Chapter Six
The Red Dragon

As Chi Fu walked slowly back past Mae's shop, he saw a sign in her window. A bright red dragon looked out at Chi Fu. It was exactly like the one he had made out of clay for Little Yu Mei. At first he thought he was dreaming; then he read the sign: "Fifty dollars reward for the best paper lantern."

He pressed his nose flat against the window and read the instructions. The paper lanterns would be judged down by the Tamsui River on

Dragon Boat Festival day—the fifth day of the fifth moon. Every year at the same time, beautiful dragon boats raced down the river. If the race made the Dragon King and his helpers happy, they would give Taiwan good weather all year; then the rice plants would grow sturdy and green and everyone would have enough money until the next crop.

Chi Fu remembered the lantern contest last year. Thousands of people had watched as contestants carried or pulled their lanterns across the stage. Some lanterns were on poles like kites, others were on wheels and were pulled across the floor. They were all beautiful and each had a candle burning inside to show off the bright colors. Lanterns could be made in any shape—birds, houses, ships, animals or butterflies—but Chi Fu would make his like a dragon.

Yes, he had already decided to make a lantern and win the contest. Then he could buy that red bicycle.

He ran home and rushed into the kitchen to tell the family about his plans.

"But the festival is only two weeks away," Grandfather Li said. "Is that enough time for you to make a prize-winning lantern?"

"Oh, yes!" Chi Fu said breathlessly. "I'll work very hard after school, and it will be beautiul—you'll see!"

Grandather Li nodded. "Yes, it must be beautiful to win. But do not forget that slow work produces fine things."

It was an especially gay supper that night. Mrs. Li gave Chi Fu and Little Yu Mei some pennies for sugar cane. They bought two long pieces and chewed the sweet juice out of them in front of Mae's store. The dragon in the poster seemed to be smiling.

In the days that followed, Chi Fu spent every free minute working on the dragon lantern. First he drew plans on a large sheet of paper. Then he collected thin bamboo sticks and cut them down to the right sizes. When he finished gluing the sticks together, he would have the skeleton of his lantern. His dragon would be on wheels so that it would roll across the stage like a boat on the water.

Everyone helped. Grandfather Li checked his plans, and Little Yu Mei held the sticks while Chi Fu glued them together. Chen Wu collected scraps of colored rice papers from his neighbors and brought them to Chi Fu. Even the chickens and duck helped by staying very quiet so the others could work harder.

Last was the most difficult part, gluing the paper onto the wooden frame. Chi Fu worked slowly and carefully; his practice with clay had taught him patience, and his fingers were sure and steady.

He had just finished gluing rice paper skin onto the spiked dragon tail when he saw Tao Chi poke his head around the bamboo fence. He had a slingshot in his hand. Chi Fu's heart raced as he stood between the precious dragon lantern and the troublemaker. Little Yu Mei was frozen on the spot, looking anxiously from one boy to the other.

When Tao Chi saw that the adults were not around, he boldly entered the yard. "Hey, stupid!" he laughed. "So now you are playing with toys!" He put a pebble into his slingshot and danced around Chi Fu, trying to aim at the lantern.

Chi Fu jumped at Tao Chi and brought

him to the ground. The two rolled over and
over, kicking and yelling and hitting.

Little Yu Mei came suddenly alive and ran
out of the yard screaming, "A fight! A fight!"

Tao Chi took one last swing at Chi Fu and

scrambled to his feet when he saw Mrs. Li come running with Little Yu Mei.

"Coward! Coward!" Little Yu Mei shouted, angrily shaking her small fist after Tao Chi.

Chapter Seven
Typhoon!

After that crisis, Chi Fu hurried to finish his lantern, since the festival was less than one week away.

The dragon's head was almost finished when the skies over Taiwan darkened.

"It must be the sleeping dragon snoring inside Grass Mountain," Mrs. Li said. "This is not the season for storms."

But it turned out to be more than the snore of a sleeping dragon. By late afternoon every bus carried a red flag to warn people that a bad storm—a typhoon—was coming to the island.

The bad weather did not frighten Chi Fu, because storms came to his island many times each year. Usually there was a big wind, plenty of rain and that was all, but this one was different and coming fast. The sky suddenly grew dark and within minutes rain pelted down—raindrops as hard as pebbles that had a sting when they struck Chi Fu's face.

Luckily, Grandfather Li had heard about the storm and came wheeling home on his bicycle just about the time the rain started in earnest. It came in sheets, and the powerful wind shoved it through windows and into doorways. Chi Fu helped bring in the bicycle, the three chickens and duck. While everyone else huddled in the kitchen, Chi Fu climbed up on the roof and took the stones Grandfather Li handed him. They had to be placed on the roof to keep the tiles from blowing away. The rain and wind blinded Chi Fu, and twice he almost skidded right off the edge of the roof.

When that job was done, they had to close the wooden shutters and nail them tight over the windows. Chi Fu was glad they had no glass in the windows, because it would surely have been broken by the force of the wind.

During the evening the wind became even stronger and tried to break down the walls and tear off the roof like some wild animal. There was no light because the wind had blown down the electric wires; only a candle glowed in the kitchen.

"We might as well go to bed," Grandfather Li finally said. "We have done all we can to protect the house."

"That's a good idea," Mrs. Li agreed. "The storm will probably blow itself out during the night."

"Let's send a message to the Broom Star," Little Yu Mei said, "and she will stop the storm."

"That's just a fairy tale," Chi Fu scoffed. "There really isn't any Broom Star in the sky who sweeps clouds away."

"Please!" Little Yu Mei begged, tugging at his sleeve. "Please let's do it—just in case."

Chi Fu sighed and helped his sister cut a large star out of brown wrapping paper and pin it behind the kitchen door. If the Broom Star got the message, she was supposed to sweep the clouds from the sky with her giant broom, and it would be a clear, sunny morning.

Chi Fu pulled the blanket up over his head and tried to sleep, but the shrieking wind kept him awake. He got up three times to see if his dragon lantern was safe in a corner of the room.

He had just dozed off when there was a terrific clap of thunder that brought him wide awake again. The wind stopped blowing for a moment, and there was an eerie silence in the house. Something was wrong. Chi Fu could feel it in his bones.

Chi Fu swung his feet over the edge of the bed and stepped down—into icy cold water.

"Aiyee!" he yelled. The rain had quietly crept under the door and covered the floor. The family awoke, and everyone splashed this way and that in the water trying to pick up things that might get wet.

Grandfather Li found a candle and lit it. They all gasped when they saw the dark water swirling up to their ankles. Chi Fu saw pieces of his lantern floating around in the water. He picked up some wet rice paper and stood looking at it for a long time. The lantern was ruined. His last chance was gone.

"You must forget the lantern now," his mother said quietly, "and help us carry our things out to higher ground."

Chapter Eight
The Rescue

The rest of the night was like a bad dream. While the rain and wind lashed their faces and soaked them through, the Li family carried their bundles up the dark mountainside to a church that stood on higher ground. Little Yu Mei stumbled and fell with almost every step, and Chi Fu's arm began to ache from holding onto her. Many of their neighbors were struggling up the mountain too, and the sound of babies crying mingled with the howling of the wind.

They all moved into the neat white church where the minister and his wife brought them hot tea and warm blankets. Every time there

was a bad storm, the church opened its doors
to everyone.

Grandfather Li looked around at all the

faces and said, "That's funny; I don't see the Chang family." Chi Fu was glad Tao Chi Chang wasn't there: a storm like this was trouble enough without a bully too. But Grandfather Li was worried, and after a word to the minister, he beckoned to Chi Fu, and they both went out into the dark night again.

"Be careful," Mrs. Li called after them with a worried note in her voice.

"Where are we going?" Chi Fu asked, trying to arrange his rubber poncho so that the wind couldn't lift it up at the corners.

Grandfather Li set out at a fast jog. "We must see what happened to Tao Chi's family; perhaps they need our help."

The storm seemed to get worse as they came closer to the side road that led to the Chang house. With heads down, they battled their way forward, ducking occasional tree branches that flew by like great birds.

Grandfather Li was right. The Changs did need help. The family was still inside the house, although the water was well over their ankles, trying to fix some sort of stretcher for Mr. Chang. He had been putting rocks on the roof when he slipped and fell down onto a wooden table, breaking his right leg. Tao Chi's white face looked up at the two as they entered the house. There was nothing of the bully in his look now, only a frightened boy.

"I'm so happy to see you," Mrs. Chang cried with tears in her eyes. "We haven't been able to get him out of the house."

"It's all right now," Grandfather Li said soothingly, "Tao Chi is a big, strong boy; he and I can support Mr. Chang while Chi Fu helps you carry your belongings."

Soon they were all slipping and struggling along the road, making their way back to the church. More than once Chi Fu staggered under the load he was carrying and fell flat in the mud.

When they arrived at the church, he was a sight. His legs and pants were plastered with mud. There was mud on his face and in his hair. Tao Chi looked almost as bad.

Grandfather Li put an arm around each boy. "You both did a fine job," he said. "I'm proud of you."

Tao Chi and Chi Fu sheepishly looked at each other, and Chi Fu wondered how long it would be before the Chang boy was his usual nasty self.

Chapter Nine
Chi Fu's Last Chance

In the morning the sun shone brightly as if nothing at all had happened. The Broom Star had done her work well; there was not a cloud in the blue sky. Water began to flow out of the houses and down to the river and rice fields.

Everyone went home to start the difficult job of cleaning up. Furniture had to be put outside to dry and the layer of mud on the floors had to be washed off. Poor Chi Fu picked up all that was left of his dragon boat lantern and threw it away.

Mrs. Li was watching him with sadness in her eyes. "I'm sorry about your lantern, but we all lost precious things in the storm."

"I know," he choked down a sob, "but I did so want to win."

The daily newspaper carried a notice that said the Dragon Boat Festival would still be held the next week. It would also celebrate the end of the storm, but Chi Fu felt that he didn't want to celebrate anything ever again.

Grandfather Li did not go to work that day or for many days to come. He had caught a bad cold out in the rain and had to stay in bed.

When Dragon Boat Festival day arrived, Chi Fu's mother said, "Why don't you take Little Yu Mei to see the festival? I will stay with grandfather."

"You can use my bicycle," Grandfather Li called from his bedroom, "and you might even try to sell some clay flowers."

At any other time Chi Fu's heart would have leapt for joy. He had always wanted to ride that bicycle into Taipei like his grandfather. But now, even the idea that his grandfather thought he was grown-up enough to ride the bicycle did not matter. He looked away. He did not want to see the lantern contest, to see all those other lanterns glowing across the stage that night.

But then, he suddenly smiled. A wonderful idea popped into his head like a firecracker going off. Perhaps there was still a chance to earn enough money to buy a red bicycle.

Chi Fu grabbed Little Yu Mei and swung her off her feet.

"All right," he laughed, "I will take her to the Dragon Boat Festival."

The family looked at him with puzzled eyes, but Chi Fu did not explain his new happiness. He sang cheerfully as he tied the little table and stool onto the bicycle just the way Grandfather Li always did. Little Yu Mei sat in front of him on the handlebars as they rode along toward Taipei. As he had promised his mother, Chi Fu got off and walked when they reached dangerous traffic on the main roads.

They joined crowds of people already gathered on the banks of the Tamsui River. There were hundreds of grandstand seats and a stage for the lantern contest built next to the river. Little Yu Mei asked him questions about his plans for the day, but Chi Fu only looked very mysterious. "It will be a surprise," he said.

The festival was in full swing. There were clowns dancing around with funny masks covering their faces, men on stilts, and hundreds of stands selling good things to eat and drink. Chi Fu's mouth watered when he saw the ice cream, red candy cherries, and sugar doughnuts.

On the sparkling river the brilliant dragon boats were ready. Each one had a magnificent

dragon head and tail that had taken months to build. Oarsmen were getting ready to push the boats through the water with bright red oars. Over in a corner a crowd of children carefully lined up their paper lanterns for the evening contest. Chi Fu did not see a single dragon. lantern. His would have been the only one and might have won the prize.

He found a shady spot on the riverbank and set up his table and chair. Then, while Little Yu Mei watched, he began to work.

Chapter Ten
Dragon Magic

He had finished one bright red dragon and looked around for a possible customer, but everyone was facing the river waiting for the race to start and not one person even glanced his way. Chi Fu was filled with worry and with hopelessness. Grandfather Li had said that people would not buy his silly dragons. Well, maybe he was right.

Little Yu Mei pointed to a figure walking fast in their direction. "Here comes someone," she said, "but I think it is—yes, it is Tao Chi."

Chi Fu watched Tao Chi come nearer. This was the bully's big chance to make fun of the clay dragon, and Chi Fu didn't even have the heart to fight back. But Tao Chi wasn't smiling; in fact, he didn't look mean at all. He stood with his hands on his hips looking at

Chi Fu and the dragon for a moment. Then he suddenly turned toward the crowd and began yelling in a singsong voice, "Hey, everybody, step right up and see the most amazing clay-boy in the world. Is he making flowers and birds? No, he is making dragons for this special day. Now who will buy the first dragon?"

A few children in the crowd heard the word "dragon" and came up to see what it was all about. Soon there was a crowd of children watching Chi Fu.

His hands flew like magic, and he finished one dragon after the other in record time. These children had never before seen a clay-boy making —of all things—colorful dragons, and they could have watched him all day. Not only that, Chi Fu told them funny stories about the Dragon King and his twenty-four helpers. The children especially liked the story about the dragon and the monkey.

"A long, long time ago," Chi Fu told the children, "a dragon and his wife were sent to live at the bottom of the sea, to keep an eye on things there for the Dragon King.

"The dragon's wife did not like living at the bottom of the sea, and she became quite ill. She got thinner and thinner, and her color faded from bright orange to pale yellow. Her husband became very worried and asked her many times what special delicacy she would like to eat.

Finally, she told him she had a terrible craving for a monkey's heart.

"The dragon swam for hours until he reached land. The first thing he saw was a tall banana tree, and there—on the topmost branch —perched a monkey. The two chattered for a while about the weather, but the monkey looked as if he was in no hurry to come down.

"The dragon smiled his best smile and said, 'Why do you stay in one tree? I know an island not far from here where you can find coconuts as big as watermelons.'

"The monkey was tired of eating bananas, and the vision of huge, juicy coconuts made his mouth water. 'I'd like to visit the island,' he told the dragon, 'but how can I get across the ocean?'

" 'That's easy,' said the dragon. 'Just get on my back and I'll take you there.'

"In no time at all, the dragon was swimming along with the monkey clinging to his back.

"When they were far out in the water, the dragon said, 'Now, please hold tight, because we are going to dive to the bottom of the sea.' He was a very polite dragon, so he explained that his wife would surely die if she did not eat the heart of a monkey.

"The monkey thought hard for a moment. Then he said, 'Illustrious friend, why didn't you tell me before? I was in such a hurry to taste those coconuts that I left my heart on top of the banana tree. If you turn back,' he promised, 'I'll be delighted to give you the heart for your wife.'

"The dragon swam back to shore, thanking his lucky stars that he had met such a kind monkey.

"He was still waiting when the moon rose over the top of the banana tree."

When he finished, the crowd around Chi Fu was laughing so hard at the silly dragon that parents began to come over to see what was going on.

"How clever of him to make dragons on Dragon Boat Festival day!" someone said.

"Yes," another said, "and what good

souvenirs they are to take home."

"I'll take one!" a voice cried; then they all wanted to buy. Chi Fu sold dragons as fast as he could make them. When the gun went off to start the boat races, Chi Fu had used all his clay and sold every dragon.

They both looked around for Tao Chi, but he was gone. "He turned out to be a nice boy after all," Little Yu Mei said happily. "We never could have sold the dragons without him."

"That's right," Chi Fu agreed, "and I didn't even get a chance to thank him."

He bought some ice cream for himself and Little Yu Mei, and they let the delicious coolness slide down their throats as they watched the dragon boats skim over the water. Every so often Chi Fu put his hand in his pocket to run his fingers over the money he had earned.

After the race they started off for home. Chi Fu still got a lump in his throat when he thought of his dragon lantern, so they decided not to watch the contest. They wheeled the bicycle into the yard just as the sky turned a purplish blue.

When Chi Fu gave the money to Mrs. Li, her mouth opened wide with surprise. There was not enough to buy a bicycle yet, but it was certainly a good beginning.

"We'll save it," Mrs. Li said, her eyes shining with pride, "and soon you shall have that bicycle."

Little Yu Mei and Chi Fu told their mother and grandfather all about the dragon race and Tao Chi's kindness.

Grandfather Li shook his head and smiled. "You may study to old age and yet have things to learn," he said. "I have learned that boys like Tao Chi can change and most surprising of all, that people will buy silly clay dragons." He rumpled Chi Fu's hair and added, "I have also learned that you are old enough and wise enough to work. You may take my bicycle into Taipei on Saturdays until I am well again."

Chi Fu could almost feel himself swell with pride, and he gave his grandfather such a bear-hug the old man groaned and said, "Aiyee! Not so hard. If you break my ribs, I won't be able to tell you how to mix the magic clay."

Grandfather Li stayed in bed for two weeks. He showed his grandson how to mix the clay— Chi Fu had known all along there was no dried dragon blood in it—and Chi Fu went to Taipei to sell his clay dragons and tell stories about all twenty-five of them. Sometimes his new friend, Tao Chi, went along to watch and help.

When Grandfather Li was well again, they both traveled into Taipei, only now Chi Fu rode on his own shiny red bicycle from Mr. Wang's store. Everywere he went, crowds of children ran out to meet him. They called him the Dragon Clay-Boy, and he became famous throughout the island of Taiwan.